Tricia Gardella

Blackberry Booties

PICTURES BY
Glo Coalson

Orchard Books • New York

Orchard Books, A Grolier Company
95 Madison Avenue, New York, NY 10016

Manufactured in the United States of America
Printed and bound by Phoenix Color Corp.
Book design by Nancy Goldenberg
The text of this book is set in 16 point Cheltenham.
The illustrations are watercolor.
10 9 8 7 6 5 4 3 2 1

Library of Congress Cataloging-in-Publication Data
Gardella, Tricia.
Blackberry booties / by Tricia Gardella ; illustrations by Glo Coalson.
   p. cm.
Summary: Mikki Jo is able to trade the blackberries she picks for what she needs to make a special present for her baby cousin.
ISBN 0-531-30184-2 (trade : alk. paper)—ISBN 0-531-33184-9 (lib. bdg. : alk. paper)
[1. Blackberries Fiction. 2. Barter Fiction. 3. Gifts Fiction.]
I. Coalson, Glo, ill. II. Title.
PZ7.G164Bl 2000 [E]—dc21 99-30881

To my Write Sisters—
Mary, Dian, Ann, Helen, Kirby, and Vivian—
always pick, pick, picking
—T.G.

For Britt, Dane, and Piper Coalson—
with love from "Auntie"
—G.C.

One, two, three in the bucket. One in the mouth. It was blackberry season, and Mikki Jo thought about her new baby cousin as she picked.

Samuel was so round and cute. Mikki Jo wanted to give him something at the family reunion next week. Something that said *Mikki Jo*. Maybe something she had made.

But Mikki Jo wasn't much good at making baby presents.

One, two, three in the bucket. One in the mouth. Mikki Jo was only good at one thing: picking blackberries.

Mikki Jo loved picking blackberries. She loved the dainty white flowers that promised the berries. She loved the smell of mint that climbed to her nose from the bottom of the patch. She even liked the huge yellow-and-black garden spiders that wove their webs from leaf to leaf. Mikki Jo always gave the webs plenty of room. She didn't want to break even one thread after all that hard spider work. Mikki Jo understood about hard work.

Blackberry picking was hard work, too, but it made Mikki Jo feel good. Mom made blackberry preserves and blackberry pies from Mikki Jo's berries. She even froze some for cobblers and ice cream—treats for winter from Mikki Jo's summer berries.

But not even ice cream made a good present for a tiny baby.

One, two, three in the bucket. One in the mouth. Mikki Jo's bucket was full again. She headed for home.

Baaaaaa. Mikki Jo heard sheep bleating. *Zzzzzzzz*. And a motor buzzing. The Lozanos must be shearing. She peeked her head through the shed door. Piles of wool dotted the wood floor. Mrs. Lozano was headed her way. She looked like a giant powder puff with legs.

"What do you do with all that wool?" Mikki Jo asked as Mrs. Lozano tossed her load onto a pile.

"Depends on who buys it," Mrs. Lozano said. "Could be made into rugs. Blankets. Sweaters. Even booties."

Mikki Jo's face lit up. "Can I buy some of your wool?"

Mrs. Lozano smiled. "We don't want your money, Mikki Jo. Take what you want."

"I want to pay," Mikki Jo insisted. "I don't have any money, but I'll trade you for these."

"Mmmm. Blackberry pie," said Mrs. Lozano, carrying her berries into the kitchen.

"Booties for Samuel," Mikki Jo whispered.

Grinning, she carted her wool home.

Mikki Jo tried and she tried, but no matter what she did to shape that wool, it still looked more like Grampa Harney's beard than a bootie.

One, two, three in the bucket. One in the mouth. The next morning, Mikki Jo thought about nothing but booties as she picked. Now her bucket was full, and she still hadn't figured a way to make them. She'd have to ask Mrs. Lozano.

On her way home, she heard sounds. They were coming from the Washingtons' front porch. *Whrrrrrrr. Whrrrrrrr.* Mrs. Washington's foot pumped up and down, spinning a wheel round and round. A pile of wool lay by her side, all combed and clean.

"It was such a lovely day, I decided to spin out here on the porch," Mrs. Washington said as Mikki Jo approached.

Mikki Jo watched the bobbin fill. "What do you do with all that string?"

"My yarn?" said Mrs. Washington. "Why, I might make it into a rug, or a blanket—"

"Or booties?" Mikki Jo interrupted.

"Booties too," said Mrs. Washington.

"I have some wool." Mikki Jo held up her bucket. "If I give you these, will you make it into yarn for me?"

Mrs. Washington smiled. "Love to," she said.

Mikki Jo handed Mrs. Washington her bucket.

"Mmmm, cobbler," said Mrs. Washington.

Mikki Jo ran home to fetch her wool.

A couple of days later, Mikki Jo brought her new yarn home. She wrapped it around her doll's foot. She wrapped it around her cat's foot. She even wrapped it around her own foot. She tried tying it. She tried weaving it. Then she finger-crocheted a long chain, but nothing Mikki Jo tried made that yarn look one bit like a bootie.

The reunion was now four days away, and she still had no present.

One, two, three in the bucket. One in the mouth. Mikki Jo's bucket was full again. She swatted at the mosquitoes that were chewing on the back of her neck and frowned. She had picked all morning and still hadn't come up with a single way for turning her yarn into booties for Samuel. Mrs. Washington had already spun the wool; Mikki Jo didn't want to ask her to do more. Maybe she'd just wind the yarn into a big ball. Babies like balls.

"Hello, Mikki Jo," Mrs. Nelson called as Mikki Jo took the shortcut through her yard. Under the big walnut tree, Mrs. Nelson's old oak rocker kept time to a rhythm. *Clickity, clickity, clickity. Clickity, clickity, clickity.*

"Mrs. Nelson!" Mikki Jo cried.

Mrs. Nelson looked up in surprise. She stopped rocking, but—*clickity, clickity, clickity*—her knitting needles never missed a beat. Mrs. Nelson was always knitting.

"What are you making today?"

"I'm knitting a sweater for my newest grandbaby," said Mrs. Nelson.

"Want some blackberries?"

"How can I take your berries?" Mrs. Nelson asked. "You've worked so hard. Just look at your arms. They're all scratched up."

Mikki Jo told Mrs. Nelson all about her new cousin Samuel.

"Mmmmm, blackberries for ice cream," said Mrs. Nelson as she carried her berries into the house.

Mikki Jo ran home to fetch her yarn.

Two days later, Mrs. Nelson handed Mikki Jo a lovely pair of booties. They were soft and yellowie-white. Perfect for a baby.

But what made them special? Just from her? Everyone else had done the work. All she did was pick the berries.

One, two, three in the bucket. One in the mouth. Before she knew it, the bucket was full again. Mikki Jo looked at her hands and sighed.

Suddenly she had an idea. She grabbed her bucket and ran all the way home.

Squish, *squish*, *squish*. Around and around. Then out in the sun to dry.

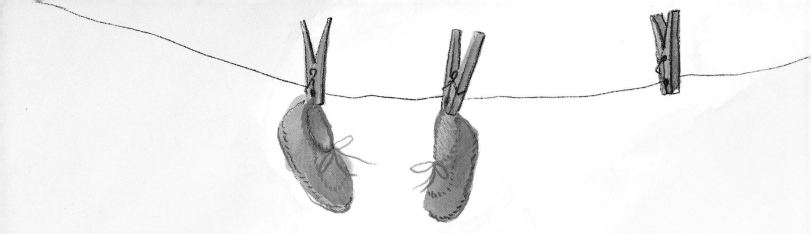

Mikki Jo rubbed her purple hands together and smiled. Blackberry booties. Just right. Finally, a perfect gift for her new cousin Samuel.